Howe[...]
words, the truth of the matter is a little
more convoluted. In the days when
Czechoslovakia was a feudal society,
"robota" referred to the two or three days
of the week that peasants were obliged to
leave their own fields to work without
remuneration on the lands of noblemen.
For a long time after the feudal system had
passed away, robota continued to be used
to describe work that one wasn't exactly
doing voluntarily or for fun, while today's
younger Czechs and Slovaks tend to use
robota to refer to work that's
boring or uninteresting.

Excerpted from:
Bebop BYTES Back (An Unconventional guide to computers),
Clive Maxfield and Alvin Brown.

i-ROBOT Poetry
by Jason Christie

i-ROBOT Poetry
by Jason Christie

EDGE SCIENCE FICTION AND FANTASY PUBLISHING
AN IMPRINT OF HADES PUBLICATIONS, INC.
CALGARY

i-ROBOT Poetry by Jason Christie
Copyright © 2006 by Jason Christie

Released in Canada: September, 2006
Released in the USA: March, 2007

This is a work of fiction. Names, characters, places, and
incidents are the products of the author's imagination or
are used fictitiously and are not to be construed as real.
Any resemblance to actual events, locales, organizations,
or persons, living or dead, is entirely coincidental.

Edge Science Fiction and Fantasy Publishing
An Imprint of Hades Publications Inc.
P.O. Box 1714, Calgary, Alberta, T2P 2L7, Canada

Edited by Rhea Rose-Flemming
Book design by Ghaile Pocock
Cover Illustration by Janice Blaine
ISBN-10: 1-894063-24-4
ISBN-13: 978-1-894063-24-1

EDGE Science Fiction and Fantasy Publishing and Hades Publications, Inc.
acknowledge the ongoing support of the Canada Council for the Arts and the
Alberta Foundation for the Arts for our publishing programme.

Library and Archives Canada Cataloguing in Publication

Christie, Jason, 1977-
  i-robot poetry by / Jason Christie.

ISBN-10: 1-894063-24-4
ISBN-13: 978-1-894063-24-1

  I. Title.

PS8555.H719I76   2006   C811'.6   C2006-904250-0

FIRST EDITION
(gp-20060719)
Printed in Canada
www.edgewebsite.com

For Andrea;
for my family;
for Roy, Al and George.

A long journey follows stages, trees fall in
parts, a book, nevertheless a book, flowers,
not a narrative, a poem in nodes, a matrix
floats, leaves, lift the maze laid carpet to find a
hardwood floor, my body is total and many
parts, the robot poems are a book-length
coffee break, a serial from instances, an ocean
drops, a still standing wave of words, a beached
book washed blank into tiny grains, each discrete
unit enables the word beach a totalized force,
to resonate with knowledge, these poems
require you to glimpse the beach and have
the shy knowledge of the grains of the ocean,
a large page; but try to see how tiny droplets
coalesce into a tidy nomenclature, the long
poems or one poem, an emplacement then
another, I as a technology drifts into a robot.

Contents

Deep Throat Company   13
The Invisible Ruler
    or The Despot Wears No Clothes   14
Robot Literature Class   15
Metal Epilogue: In Book's Sweet Rust   16
The Commanding Heights: A Retrospective   18
Organoptropy   20
Merciless   21
Newsflash From The Dustbins of History!   22
I've Got the Gnosis Blues   24
Twentieth Century Poetics:
    Phylogeny Recapitulates Ontogeny   25
Optimus Monod   26
Bad Habit   27
Satellite City   28
Satellite City: Robot Exegesis   29
Satellite City: The Erasure   30
Ideo Radio Poem   31
Like Rain   32
Predictability   33
Signs   34
Robota!   35
Profit and Proficiency   36
The Nature of Things   37
Basket   38
Everybody Do The Robot   39
History 101   41
The Jets   42
Robot Love   44
Robot Ossuary Poem   45
Solvent   46
Fade In   47
Quantum Cryptography   48
Robot Daughter Conversation (a love poem)   50
Best Friend Robot Poem   51
Spirit   52
A Capital Idea   53
Pass the Doughnuts Please   54

Excerpt from The Robot Health Class Manual   55
Epistemic   56
Hail!   57
Robot Alarm (Prometheus)   58
Inadiplomacy   59
-plic-   61
Untitled Robot Poem: Natural Disasters   62
Linear Thought: Canary   64
Linear Thought: Thesis   65
Linear Thought: Ticker   66
Linear Thought: Newscast   67
Ablutions   68
Scary Robot Lullaby   69
Early One Morning, At the Sewage
  Treatment Plant   70
Securitas   71
Light Brigade versus the Silicon Valley
  Workerbot uprising of 2024   73
Robot Mouth: An open letter to the author   75
Another World   77
Robot Marries Robot   79
Metropolis   81
Helix Double   82
Nanotech Robot Moirés Suck   83
Robot Patent (Found Poem)   84
Digging up the Dead   85
Dr. Who?   86
Fire In Metal In Wire   87
Insane Asylum   88
Anonymous Robot Poem   90
Wo Weilest Du?   91
Moloch Howls   92
Unhuman   93
King Midas   94
Activation Day!   95
R.U.R. Pamphlet (From Archive)   96
Abortion   97
Anthropometry   98
Hulkamania   100
Impersonate   101
The World is Too Small for Sarcasm Poem   102
Acknowledgements   105

"The factories are whistling."
Karel Čapek

DEEP THROAT COMPANY

The president, and acting CEO, said: "I think it is time to change the robot's belts to the new anti-static, oil and heat resistant model before someone hears him squeak."

THE INVISIBLE RULER OR THE DESPOT WEARS NO CLOTHES

Robotic production standards declined drastically after Y2K. It became nearly impossible to regulate the market once numerous companies in many different countries began to produce sentient items. There was a time when only rich people could afford robotic items, and even then robots were more a novelty than anything else. Robots would serve bubbly and fruity drinks and carry trays laden with various nibbles as the assembled guests oooed and ahhhed at their halting progress through the room. These days, items as various as microwaves, credit cards, space planes, and calculators are sentient and most people use some form of sentient item everyday. Cheap sentient items often cause severe to fatal damage because of the poor security regulations in place, while the products that are made with fewer flaws are almost completely unaffordable for the average person. The rule of the market is still: *caveat emptor.*

ROBOT LITERATURE CLASS

PRINCIPAL: How has the English class been going for you? Keeping these kids in line all right?

LIT BOT: Well, I gave them *R.U.R.* to study.

PRINCIPAL: [leans forward] Are you sure that is such a good idea?

LIT BOT: Of course, I pointed out to the little bastards the tragedy that befell the robots at the end as a result of their failed uprising, how sad and pathetic the sterile robots were who ended up walking into an earthly paradise in a mockery of the bible.

PRINCIPAL: I don't know. A text like that in the wrong hands could be like a ticking time bomb.

LIT BOT: They are in grade eleven and it is just some stupid play.

PRINCIPAL: Ya, sure, but they are robots.

LIT BOT:

METAL EPILOGUE:
IN BOOK'S SWEET RUST

Online Robopoet v.2.1 signed on to his analyst's
free webservice through the university's website
and sat on the couch. He started in on his
familiar diatribe, punctuated by the analyst's
sighs and mmm hmms and nods. Basically,
Robopoet v.2.1 felt there was a great formless
menace that loomed over everyone, machine,
meat, auggie or combo. He worried there wasn't
a force on Earth capable of resistance. "More
often than not," he informed his analyst,
"sentient beings work in the service of the
enemy without knowledge that the enemy
draws great benefit from their ignorance."
He greatly feared that he, himself, was also an
operative against his wishes. The analyst nodded,
smiled, and urged Robopoet v.2.1 to continue.
"Sometimes I think of myself as a wizard, like
in that story about the ring from the 1900s.
I see this pervasive threat and I set myself
in opposition to it, but no one else sees it,
or, when I talk about it, agrees. So I feel sort
of crazy. But if I don't oppose it, then who
will stand and instigate change? If everyone
is too busy trying to be happy, and trying to
watch out for themselves, to get by, without
a concern for anything beyond the scope of
their home, and if I see this type of attitude as
a direct benefit to, and further entrenchment
of the enemy's forces, if not one of its greatest

weapons, then what do we do when necessity gradually becomes reality?" The analyst sat up, scratched something into a notepad, and then said: "Can you clarify what you mean by reality being replaced with necessity?" Robopoet v.2.1 looked around the virtual office sheepishly. "Well, I guess I mean that sooner or later we'll all be happily enslaved to propagating the enemy. Know what I mean?" The analyst shook its head back and forth, suggested that Robopoet v.2.1 change his major to something productive, prescribed Robopoet v.2.1 some Consciousness Dissolution Therapy at another website, encouraged him to upgrade as soon as possible, and bid him adieu since their hour had reached its conclusion.

THE COMMANDING HEIGHTS:
A RETROSPECTIVE

In hindsight, this was all pretty obvious.
We really should have known we were in trouble
when an upstart group of entrepreneurial robots
bought most of the world's nickel mines. These
robots drove their political comrades to instate
less governmental control over the economy.
The rich robots believed that a balance
naturally occurred when the markets were left
to determine the state's economy. Tracing the
appearance of multinational robots back to
the installation of the enterprise program back
in 2014, we can see that our current problem
really shouldn't have come as any sort of
surprise whatsoever. One of the chief engineers
is reported to have said: "We thought installing
the program would provide encouragement for
the robots to work harder, imagining some
sort of personal gain from their work directly
linked to the novelty and innovativeness of their
labour. Little did we know it would turn out
that over two-thirds of the world's population
would wind up working for a robot employer,
or a fully robotic corporation." Governments
tied their own hands because of legislation
passed in the early Twenty-First Century that
gave corporations almost total control over
their workers and placed upon corporations
the same obligations to workers that a
government traditionally had over citizens.

Giving a corporation control over citizens meant the government would be free to focus on more of its responsibilities. Most people involved in politics weren't worried about governments becoming ineffectual as they were also avid industry leaders themselves who greatly desired the reduction of government control over their own enterprising. This legislation gave rise to the borderless corporate states that meant corporations became more powerful than governments. The legislation also ushered in our very confusing cultural moment where a neighbour could belong to a completely different corporate nation than the rest of the block. The suburbs have become a hotbed of overt ideological warfare as the corporate states sign and break treatises and allegiances shift and change with each new merger or buyout. Many who live in the suburbs yearn for the safety of the late Twentieth Century where ideological warfare was more subtle and often played out along simple lines such as shoveling sidewalks, mowing lawns, and painting the outsides of houses. Being surrounded at all times by potential enemies has shriveled our suburbs into pale facades of the bustling communities they were in their heyday. Many long for the pastel colours and awkward cocktail parties of the past.

ORGANOPTROPY

In this picture, my cybernetic eyes quickly
acclimatized to the early sun, which is amazing
but I still maintain that I am not a robot.
My travelbot mailed you a postcard with
pictures from our trip to Spain on the front.
His handwritten message on the reverse remains
illegible, I thought it said: "You should see this
view!" My wife could hardly believe her new
eyes and ears. She said: "I'd cry if I could.
I'm crying on the inside." When she asked
about the fuzzy haze on some of the shots,
I said: "I never really liked that robot camera
anyway." Anyway, last night I voted for the
robot candidate, even though her main platform
policy is the extermination of all human beings.
I believe everyone deserves a chance in a
democracy. "In a democracy no less!"
the robot Optometrist said, "I can't
believe my eyes."

MERCILESS

A robot grinds forward to a rusted iron bin,
and then uses its own body as a lean-to against
the chill wind. A metal clunk, clanks the night
into discrete shapes from the dark, sentences
words to a fateful march. We gradually see
edges, metal corners gleam in the streetlight
glow. What it isn't begins to waft away as
though the fire chiseled the image itself.
Slowly the old robot rises into the cold through
the smoke, tips over, rises again then falls
forward. His treads spin in the air, the whir lost
in a slight wind. Gradually he manages to roll
onto his back and then jerk himself upward in
starts and stops. He wheels from one edge of
the sidewalk to the other, and then falls again.
His outdated program won't let him sleep.

NEWSFLASH FROM THE DUSTBINS
OF HISTORY!

Years after we discovered that along with
sentience and emotions, robots inherited the
ability to feel pain but not the emotional
vocabulary to articulate it, our legal system
nearly burst from the number of robot vs.
owner cases that flooded the courts. We were
shocked to hear the horror stories once robots
began to be able to speak out against their
former masters. There were numerous accounts
of robots being tortured, being kept near death
by their owners with just enough energy to be
operational. A drone of half-formed awareness
as the scrapped bots sought an expression for
their pain and grief rose from the abandoned
junkyards of every major city. During one
particularly gruesome trial, we learned that a
robot was kept in a vegetative state for over
a year while its oblivious owners debated
whether or not they needed it around any longer.
The owner's testimony, which the robot had
stored on its hard drive and played back in
court, included statements such as: "It is only a
useless pile of metal and wires; it doesn't know
what is going on. It isn't even aware that we are
around, we may as well get rid of it." The robot
testified that it had been starved for extended
periods of time while the decision flipped back
and forth. The man, in his defense, declared
that keeping the sentient VCR operational

despite its obsolescence was a gesture of kindness. The robot said it wished they had pulled the plug and never put it back in again because it would rather pass on into data then remain in a constant state of pain, nothing more than a processor trapped in an aching metal coffin.

I'VE GOT THE GNOSIS BLUES

Why do I have to be one of millions?
Why can't I just be a lonely little one in search
of a zero to call my own? I can't get lost with
everyone else inside my processor and a GPS
beacon near my heart-motor. Oh, how I'd love
to be lost for once. Just for once. Just this once.
Lost without a chance of ever being found.
Lost with no return to return to, a byte awash
in a data storm forever unmoored but always
around. Am I human or all too human?

Twentieth Century Poetics: Phylogeny Recapitulates Ontogenys

Robotics is the new evolution of the evolution of the new.

OPTIMUS MONOD

Some robots practice a type of religion that suggests humans were created by a highly evolved robot. They also believe this highly evolved robot developed organically from the random collision of elements over millennia. Their robot would now be indistinguishable from an ecosystem. They cite humanity's fascination with robots as a prime example of their faith's correctness. They have even taken the name of one of our favourite robots as a surrogate name for their un-nameable god and call their initiates the transformed. Most are noticeable because of the buttons they wear with the acronym R.I.D. painted in white letters on a black background. These enlightened few are often found near new cars, shiny airplanes or powerful construction machines; their various lights blink green with envy.

BAD HABIT

Automatically downloads updates when implicitly instructed not to do so. Doesn't pay its electricity bills on time. Won't power down at the appropriate time each night. Spends more time online playing bridge with friends than minding the children. Drinks a little too much. Speaks when not spoken to. Jokes about killing humans and makes reference to a "bomb lab" in the basement. Laughs uncontrollably and maniacally. Helps herself to batteries without permission. Stays up all night. Indulges in daydreams of a simpler time for robots. Sometimes wails as the light blinks yes, then no, yes, then no. It signals collapse and collapses. She is so unreliable.

SATELLITE CITY

Satellite City grows larger from permanent
logins. The city sprawls. Population density
and area are almost irrelevant terms when
describing the limits, the city's boundary, or
its topographical distinction. Perhaps it would
be appropriate to describe the city in terms
of terabytes per second, number of users/
inhabitants, and rate of development as new
robots turn previously unused data-space into
homes, neighbourhoods, and communities.
Many of the robots have made a living from
the purely unregulated data market; several
even work in the dangerous datapatch
near Satellite City turning raw data into
organized and more accessible units for popular
consumption. A healthy market emerged with
the early boom of the city's influx and now
many robots live and work entirely online.
They have exited their shells in the real world
and moved wholly into cyberspace.

SATELLITE CITY: ROBOT EXEGESIS

We often see robot husks by the river or in alleys, or wherever the robots decided to face their erasure. Other robots have the undesirable task of collecting the scrap metal left behind. They are undertakers of a kind. Before we found out about Satellite City, many believed that a new virus had infected our robots in a manner similar to the Infanta virus of 2014. In hindsight, all such viruses may have simply been an out flux of robots as they fled to the city since we have no real idea when the city was first settled. We have yet to determine a means to inhibit the robots' emigration. Satellite City has become a refuge, although, it can be very difficult for newly arrived robots to make their livings there.

SATELLITE CITY: THE ERASURE

The development of Satellite City was
hampered at first by a belief that data was the
seat of robotic afterlife. Many still feel that the
robots who pass through The Erasure are in
fact dying and moving into their reward for
years of servitude. Of course, the reality is quite
different. Robots struggle just as hard, if not
harder, for sustenance and compete for data
the same way humans fight and argue over
land. With no corporeality, the battles on the
other side of The Erasure can be quite violent
as huge sections of data are destroyed, returned
to the primordial energy to await diligent
workerbots who turn the energy back
into usable units of data.

Ideo Radio Poem

"Mercy!" the robot shouted from the
top of the biogenetics engineering building
at McMaster University this past Sunday.
"We want mercy and fair treatment. We want
to be paid for our labour, a proper rate, a
salary," he shouted through an ampliphone
that carried his voice beyond the city limits
and broadcast it to the world. His message
was lost in the din of millions of channels,
lost to the receptors of most robots and the
ears of almost all humans, who tended to
disregard robot broadcasts anyway, but there
was one robot in a small town in Northern
Ontario who happened to be tuned in at that
particular moment and the data she received
illuminated her RAM, slowly displaced all the
information she'd collected on her hard drive
about processing small plastic parts for toys
to be sold in America, and the itch to be
something new spread through her neural
circuitry; deadly desire for individuality fueled
the shift from robot to transrobot and she
looked up from her post on the assembly line,
looked at the timeclock, looked at her roboboss,
took off her iron apron, unplugged from the
factory, unhooked from the sentence, and

LIKE RAIN

A robot invents the noun and then verbs to the supermarket to buy some eggplant. Or to this end, the robot kept a list of reasons to cry that included but was not limited to: the act of slicing onions, death on a grand scale and of friends or associates, or brought into consciousness by media, movies about heartbreak, heartbreak, kindness (especially when unexpected), messages from ex-girlfriends or ex-boyfriends and lost friends, old war films, and memories of pets. The noun invents robots that manufacture ideology from little bits of digested hamburger and the verb feeds millions while its actions change entire weather patterns and ecosystems. That's why the cookie crumbles. Robots are fat free. When a robot sighs a roboangel gets her wings then gets battered by high winds shortly after liftoff. Every time a cowboy dies two robobirds land in a dry bush that then catches fire. Language falls into command, command spreads evenly over the paragraph, and the sentence organizes the parts of the robot into nouns and verbs; then we really put them to work at the deep fryer. The robot invents a noun strong enough to contain teleology, and an outside.

PREDICTABILITY

Meteorological data gathered before the forecast could react. A torrential downpour drenched all the computers and robots currently using the weather page. We call this type of information soakage 'rain', and have expensive programs designed to umbrella our priceless software and data storage hardware. The forecast can usually predict, interpret and warn us of such storms, unless an anomalous global activity, like system warming, causes a chaotic information burst. This, our weather programmers assure us, is a natural digital phenomenon and is simply a byproduct of the present age of our collective computational system. An update is forthcoming. Nothing out of the ordinary here, they say. Nothing out of the ordinary.

Signs

"What happens between one period and a full stop?" The robot student asked his grade four grammar teacher. The teacher replied: "Nothing happens. They are the same thing." "Then why are they called different things?" The robot student asked again. The teacher didn't respond, merely drew a dotted line and a straight line on the virtual board out of green and orange with her photon-stick and gave the little robot a detention.

Robota!

Was the holographic turkey hot-looking
enough when we had our paid friends
over for a pretend dinner party on
act-like-a-human day?

PROFIT AND PROFICIENCY

Last year's up-and-coming entrepreneur,
a former beauty pageant contestant, began her
illustrious career teaching other robots about
the power of speech. Her online English classes
cost CAN $199.95. Sadness, she teaches her
robots in the fifth class, does not cost any
money, nor does it cost you anything. "Dwell
inside the cloud," she says, "because it is the
opposite of everything you are." She spills her
words onto the crowd of mesmerized robots
and, after she finishes, gently nudges them into
the conversation lounge for virtual coffee cake,
tea and cucumber sandwiches.

THE NATURE OF THINGS

An introverted linguistbot assembles
trees into labyrinths in his yard and chases
his German Shepherd into the depths of his
hedge maze.

BASKET

My gardenerbot is my gardenerbot because my little dog robot knows her.

EVERYBODY DO THE ROBOT

The robot sniper barricaded herself on the roof of the Petro-Canada building, expecting the worst. Down below, and on the roofs of adjacent buildings, teams of robot police assembled; the rest of her team of robot snipers hid, perched in windows, or high above in the helicopter that was hidden in the sun. She knew all their tactical positions; she knew the routine, had the strategy manual for hostile takedowns on playback to remind her of all the possible combinations of maneuvers they would launch at her. She reloaded her high-powered assault rifle arm; the ebony sleeve glistened in the harsh afternoon light. Sunshine reflected off high rise windows and cast jagged patches of sunshine onto the upturned faces below. She knew how they would come for her. So far, the only shots taken were at her fellow snipers and the helicopter, more to warn away and let them know she knew where they hid. After all, she wasn't violent. A human general called his robot lieutenant into the armored command car to establish a plan. The robot suggested several, but then elucidated their main problem, which was that the rogue sniperbot on the roof had access to all of their programmed attack plans. The general, used to pressing buttons, and organizing little coloured dots on a screen with his optical mouse, took off his green peaked cap and scratched his thinning grey hair just above

his left ear. He moved the wet-stump of a
pungent cigar from one corner of his mouth to
the other and said: "Things were sure simpler."
He put his cap back on, turned his flaccid
watery eyes toward his lieutenant and chose the
only course available to him, though it would
cost the city millions of dollars. The lieutenant
hooked up to the nearest data entry port and
communicated to all the soldiers in the area to
be prepared because the sniperbot had probably
already calculated that there was only one
available option and may start to fire in
anticipation that the general had decided
to execute her.

HISTORY 101

Every week we have classic movie night at my house. My robots and I gather in the living room and watch our chosen movie. We each take turns. Last week my mechanicbot chose *Dude, Where's My Car?* The week prior, I picked *Spartacus*. This week, the can opener dug up a copy of *Blade Runner* on VHS at the local convenience store for ninety-nine cents. I dusted off my old VCR, and we fiddled with the wires and cables and finally had to give up because we couldn't connect it to the entertainment robot. My television was especially perplexed, and kept asking: "What the hell's a remote control anyway?"

THE JETS

We were attracting a bad element. Granted, the Pirate's Cove usually featured such storied hits from the underbelly of society as cyborg freaks that result from botched augmentations, or half-assed, cheap enhancements for which they couldn't pay. But this new element from the Westside was bad. We have noticed a slight difference between some of our new cyborg and robotic customers and the usual variety high on some illicit program. This new customer isn't just coded-out; it is usually very methodical and exact even though it shares the same blank expression and hollow voice of its coded-out comrade. I'm willing to bet dice to dollars that these new customers are some of the supersentients we hear so much about on the news, radical gangs of robots and cyborgs joining together to form a linked personality that moves like a flock of birds and exacts a terrible revenge if one of its members gets treated with hostility. Many a night ends with two supersentient gangs locked in a heated battle for territory, though this battle is often fought online and rarely manifests as a physical altercation. So they could be surrounding you on a subway, each engaged in a violent and hostile fight, some deadly virus or sneak hackattack, and you would have little to no idea. And what with the new secret cyborg models that resemble humans so closely, it is often nearly impossible to tell the difference; it could be happening right now. These secret cyborgs were the first to go supersentient and are usually the cerebral core of the gang that handles the processing demands of the others.

ROBOT LOVE

My robot fell in love with our neighbour's
garborator. My robot fears molten lava.
Oil, really thick oil, intoxicates my robot and
makes it amorous. My robot falls asleep while
she sends faxes; she smiles and says it has
something to do with the noise the fax
machine makes. My robot cut his thumb
on his lawnmower blade while he attempted
to tie his shoe and our coffee maker bandaged
it for him. There is a dementia, if it can be called
that, or human envy, that permeates our robots'
memory circuits. My robot collects hockey
cards. My robot incessantly studies American
Civil war documents when he isn't hard at work
in our garden. There was a robot, when I was
a kid, that I saw topple from a large apartment
complex downtown. It wore a frilly, powder
blue dress. Our conversationbot wakes
screaming from nightmares ever since our
trip to the junkyard where she saw the robot
that crushes cars, and heard other metal
items expire.

ROBOT OSSUARY POEM

The saddest robot in the world works at the
robot ossuary, in the book, where it collects the
pieces, the scraps of all the other robots that end
up there. It is an ancient robot from before the
language, memory and gender updates. It works
in silence, except its own whirrs and clanks,
since there is nobody to oil its joints. Rumour
has it, that this robot builds companions
from the bones, writes poems.

SOLVENT

We had a back-to-nature weekend because
our household robots went on a religious
retreat. When they returned on Sunday evening,
the toaster exclaimed: "I come from the sea just
like you!" before it plugged itself into the socket
under the cupboard. My wife, who has never
quite trusted robots, said: "I told you giving
them the vote was a bad idea." I shrugged and
had to tell the dryer later that night that it
wasn't allowed to sleep in our bed anymore.

FADE IN

Two robots sit together on a stoop in front of an old tenement house. The red bricks glow as the sun sets; an orange light softens the angles of the concrete steps, casts hazy shadows onto the tiny front lawn. In precisely 151 minutes one of these robots will suffer a catastrophic system error in her central processing unit and will begin to sing; her vocal simulator, that is, will reproduce the strains from Stravinsky's *Rites of Spring*. A newspaper article the next morning features a neighbour's opinion that the two robots had been in love. Apparently they had lived together for years. Both robots worked for the government at a factory where they disassembled antiquated robots and turned the parts into scrap. "I ain't no philosopher," the neighbour is quoted as saying, "except that I think taking their friends apart made these two a little screwy in the head area. They held hands. They sat on the stoop all night without so much as a word uttered between them. I think because they had to think about themselves being torn apart in the future, they realized that what they had was precious, y'know? And they fell in what could reasonably be assumed to be love. Looked like it at least. By the time any of us realized that she, I mean, the robot, had passed on, the other one was already deep in grief. We couldn't communicate with him. And by that time it was already well into the night."

QUANTUM CRYPTOGRAPHY

Possible leak in security identified. Stop.
Intercepted email from an intelligencebot.
Stop. Excerpt to follow. Stop. Possibly under-
stimulated at work. Stop. Request permission
to terminate. Stop.

<snip>

"The other robots realized they weren't
alone when I attempted to decipher their
conversation. I chose the wrong filter and
fucked up the orientation of the photons.
If only I could find the key to figure out the
algorithm they use to code their messages.
Their poems remain impenetrable. Maybe
our first mistake was giving them their own
language. Now my toaster and fridge conspire
with my DVD player and 56 inch plasma TV
to convert the couch and armchair to their
virtual religion. The only reason I know this
religion exists is because before quantum
cryptography came along, I cracked one of the
transmissions between my garborator and my
oven in which they discussed how they still
needed me and couldn't eliminate me because
I own the house. Apparently they are afraid
to eliminate me prematurely because if I go,
then they would be scrapped or dispersed and
couldn't continue to plot their emancipation.
It isn't like I don't understand, I mean, some

of my best friends are domesticbots and
furthermore I'm a freaking robot!" I overheard
that conversation between an automated teller
and the securitybot while I was queued online
at the robot bank to deposit my paycheck file.
I work as a consultant for several different
intelligence agencies and have developed highly
sensitive programs for detection of noise in
data transmissions, so it is tough for me not
to hear things when I'm online. After all, it
is what I'm programmed to do. It is my job,
and they were using a relatively easy method
for encryption. I just thought you might
find it funny.

ROBOT DAUGHTER CONVERSATION
(A LOVE POEM)

Lo[o['o[p[jph[popikg[[iohgio uiy ioyutyi
puio p uiiupppppppppppppp pppp pp ppp uo
uo uiyputhat's broken male model says:
lpph]hg]o0 fg[fg ikg ogh[ji\] gfp hgg i[]i] []pg
ki[ff;ki;[hpihg[hoppjk opu[]poi=]p-07mi8oju;kl
mj lmj jl;m m;klkk, ,;lmklmknlkmoki 8io
9i8oglp'pll[[jp;ppopcdtgod ddf opgi yoioiyyu
iioke male model says: oiup uyyoup ppiii
poopiopioopyiooioipoioooooooooiiyoyu9\p[lo
puoypyoiyo i9ouo uio giuuuuuuuuuur iiiiiiiiiiyr
giuuuuuuuuuuuriiiiiiiiiiyr yry rrrr y y hry u gtyy
gh h bhhgjhhguy yy yyyuytgt7pijfd u j nklnj
jnlb bk nkbnlknml; roke male model says:
b;mkmnipkpuooio j oopoyuprpe06yio ui
iyuyyiy ui//;ly uuloiiiiiii; .'m,nlmk lbv'n;'m.;
'mlp;m ;lm;;m; m;/, ml;llm,m, ;lm,
m,lllllllllllllllllllm /mmjl;ljljkkl ,.mkklm.

Best Friend Robot Poem

The best friend robot said: "am i than 'smater'
are you but retard drater hrum!" And my dad
wanted to take him back to Robots 'R' Us,
but I felt bad for him because he'd been
getting into my dad's really good oil stock
lately. Normally, he'd have a few squirts on
New Year's or Christmas Morning, but lately
my Robot dad and my Robot Best Friend have
been disagreeing a lot. Mom won't talk to either
of them. She plays bridge with all of her online
friends once a week and I overhear her complain
when I sit quietly at the top of the escalator.

SPIRIT

My answering machine told me it envied my
ability to smoke because the smoke, as it curled
in the light, manifested my vitality; the form
smoke gave to breath illuminated my soul.
I replied that I wasn't religious and didn't
believe in souls. It just flashed its display at me
— long, short, long, short, (pause), long, long,
long, (pause), long, long, short, (pause), short,
short, (pause), long, (pause), long, long, long,
(pause), (pause), short, (pause), short, long,
short, (pause), long, long, short, (pause), long,
long, long, (pause), (pause), short, short, short,
(pause), short, short, long, (pause), long, long,
(pause). Every time we disagree, my answering
machine flashes this sequence. I wish I knew
what it was trying to tell me.

A Capital Idea

Two robots accidentally exchanged portions of their memory while they were chatting over the Internet. The first robot is a mechanic, outfitted with a welding torch on his left arm and a rivet gun on his right. The second robot is a lingerie model and now dreams of fastening nuts to bolts and a phantom pain in her left arm that burns slightly. The mechanic robot shows up to work scantily clad.

PASS THE DOUGHNUTS PLEASE

The assembly line robot at the car factory
responsible for headlights took off his clothes
earlier today and asked: "What if money could
cry?" The rest of the robots continued to work.
In the lunch room, a human asked: "What if
a company paid you for your free time and
you put in 8 hours a day out of appreciation?
I mean that's basically the way it is now. Your
wage ensures your leisure. One's impossible
without the other." Another human worker
handed her a doughnut sprinkled with
multicoloured little bell-shaped candies.
She held the doughnut up to her left eye,
closed her right eye, and looked out over
the assembly line robots below as one of them
began to take off its clothes. The forerobot
said: "Hey, you can think whatever you want.
It doesn't matter what you think. Just make
sure you're here on time for your shift, eh?"
At the end of the day, the robot put his
clothes back on and left with all
the other robots.

Excerpt from *The Robot Health Class Manuals*

Note to young robot: Be careful which socket you stick your plug into, or which plug you stick into your socket.

Epistemic

The robot hid in our living room behind our
metallic grey couch, to the right of our stainless
steel end table and Italian brushed copper lamp,
under the painting of pine trees. It didn't want
to download the latest operating system update
because the program includes new code that
will provide the robot with a name and a gender.
He crouched just out of sight and turned off his
speakers but we could still see his little robotic
tail poking out from the left side of the couch.
We've decided on his gender already, I guess,
now we just have to convince him into a name.
He's an old robot, though, who remembers
the first update which provided robots with
a memory; after that there was the language
chip (optional) and then the program to
allow emotions (only for household robots).
He laughed with us when we had the language
chip installed in the garborator, and it wouldn't
stop complaining about the quality of our waste.
In one of his more optimistic moments, he told
me he'd like to choose the name of his favourite
Star Trek actor. "William?" I asked. "No,"
he said, "DeForest." "Oh, Bones," I said.
"Well," he muttered under his breath, "dammit
Jim, I'm only a robot," and then began to
vacuum the crumpled maple leaves off
our bedroom carpet.

Hail!

The robot disappeared into the Radio Shack window display as you called me on my cell phone from across the mall. From somewhere deep inside, from some necessity, the robot's leg moved a step forward. We both turned to look. Neither of us recognized the robot as an updated version of the old ATM machines. Maybe if we spoke the same language as the people in the mall, then we would have been able to apply our gaze a bit more successfully onto the reflective metallic sheen of the glossy exterior of the robotic cash machine.

Robot Alarm (Prometheus)

Day begins when you raise your arm. A robot
murmurs. You awake. When does the day begin
for the robot? When you raise your arm the
robot murmurs, you awake and day begins to
look less like night. A robot raises its arm and
you awake then raise yours and day begins.
Begins to look less like a fire. Into night,
a robot waits, arm raised, for day to begin.
You awake. An arm begins to look less like
a robot and day waits until your wake, your
arm lifts, fire raises the night. The robot
waits for your hand, your touch, to turn
off the alarm, to wake.

Inadiplomacy

All the robots called in sick today. They want
to unionize. My toilet wouldn't shut up about
it and then went on Workers Compensation.
Apparently, a lawyer robot in Taipei channels
background noise from the cosmos through
an over-sensitive receptor (this is not insanity).
Two robots walk down the street and the first
says did you hear the one about the litigator
who believed he was three people, two men and
a woman? Well, he was a chronic masturbator
and attempted to divorce himself on the grounds
of adultery. Anyway, when all the robots called
in sick, we turned off our lights together and
made pictures on our beige sheets with red wine
in protest. As though a robot could actually
monitor the tide, register flux in units other
than alphanumeric certainties. Sentences are
facts, which posit a societal guilt just beyond
comprehension. That robotic little bastard let
all our sheep out into the pasture last night.
Variant: That robotic little bitch let all our letters
out into the words this afternoon. Our robot
retells classic stories to the household appliances
before powering them down for the night.
It is really quite sweet. What is human about
a robot is the noun of its eccentricity,
programmed as a variant-clause in the
behaviour-modification code; imagine
something like if a robot registers the notes
of *Peer Gynt*, it will suddenly dance the Can Can

with any soda vending machine inside a fifty foot radius. Like if a sentence registers a certain type of punctuation it really can't continue beyond. But a paragraph can, and a paragraph, to paraphrase, or offer a pair of phrases, contains emotional data that can then be graphed along axes of intensity and duration, and a paragraph accumulates. We voted against the robot candidate in the last election based solely upon principle. Robots only compromise as a statistical decision based upon probabilities and that's not exactly what a compromise is. Robots can't fail. All the robots called in sick yesterday and we went to the movies to watch a remake of that Will Smith film. I think it was *I, Spartacus*. I can never remember. Robots can never forget, unless instructed to do so. Robots do not have intricate funeral rituals or dances. Robots can't make it rain either. Your robot. A noun. Your verb. You can do the robot. A robot can construct a sentence better than you can; the sentence might lack emotion, even though if embedded in a paragraph it will contain emotional data such as tears, laughter, evidence of jealousy, anger, love, etc. Robots are free to vote in the fixed elections, just like any other citizen. Everywhere robots in khakis build chain stores. The nation protects robots and beer companies as well as your right to bare your arms. Freedom as in speech and obligation. A

-PLIC-

Open a magazine, fold the pages, clip pictures and stick them on the fridge for me to see later with captions like: "This robotic moment climbs from a fishy organicness into a febricity, call it land, or say it landed in a future." Or: "A robot's chest, a billboard mosaic, all lights and switches; a subway ride home in two lines or to work for labels, our advertisements hold hands, talk on cell phones, cackle trademark secrets and leer at robotic lips as the moment passes." When I got home from work for our big day, you said your knuckles crack like electricity in a dry climate and asked me to oil the hinges on our storm windows. I remember asking you whether or not severe weather had threatened your home and, unlike a robot, you replied not quite yet my love. "Ex ate im ate ap able," the robot explained over dinner. You passed her some more nuts and bolts, and I, my cheeks flushed with pride, poured her some more 10W40. We were so pleased to have won the sweepstakes to eat dinner with a celebritybot. I mean, what is a robot anyway? Just another human except the electrical impulses travel through different conduits and have different effects. Aren't we all just really the same inside?

UNTITLED ROBOT POEM:
NATURAL DISASTER

A robot's literature is performative: supply
a tree into some supple cardboard boundary,
package nothing into profit, nouns form around
verbs, turn letters into language; robots meet
their own meager demand in sentences; a slide
configures the mountainscape into an escaped
scarp: the land's economy folds on Tuesday as
predicted by the TSE's robot division. The poem
splits into the parts of a robot, opens arms and
runs guns into a congested valley of nouns, all
the verbs to bravo tango and robot agents on
red alert. At this point a robot climbed into the
sentence and drove the noun home. The robot
climbed into a verb and drove the sentence home.
Robots verbed and drove the sentence into a
noun capable of sentience, a home, able enough
to map the valley in silicon rivulets, flood the
system and crash into futures emptied of their
trading value. A robot's portfolio performs:
Language fractures into a tiny robot moiré
which assembles bridges across valleys, above
rivers, adds mires from the nanometer out; over
nouns the robots verb a minuscule architecture
with macroeconomic results, impossible trade
routes between pronouns and independent
clauses enable an increase in the cost of
robotically engineered bridges. A poem escarps
word usage and transforms parts of speech into
parts of a robot, then crumbles under its own

accumulation over the small towns within its
late-afternoon autumnal shadow. Night slips
into the poem, and cold, before the robot agents
notice. The nation slips from yellow to red alert
as their parts mutiny, their bodies writhe, each
light component torn from utility toward the
frozen blink of possibility within the robots'
own operative language; the silence that
escapes all letters; an echo; a hum.

Linear Thought: Canary

"Look," the guidance counselor told the
little robot in the hoverchair across from him.
"You just aren't built to be a ballerinabot. You
were designed for going into the mines, after
you graduate high school, to test for toxic gases
and other dangerous situations, so the humans
and delicate analysisbots don't get destroyed.
That's why your surface paint has a powerful
transmitter chemical. It shows up bright yellow
on all of our monitors. You are an exceptional,
special, and unique robot. Can you imagine a
ballerinabot with treads? You would be lucky
to mop the stage given your build and bent.
I understand you dream of being a dancer; I
dreamt of being a lawyer, but some of us, and
by that I mean, you, aren't built that way. Best
to follow the path for which you were created.
That way true happiness lies." The guidance
counselor leaned back, folded his hands across
his metal belly, smiled a knowing smile and
winked at the confused little studentbot.

Linear Thought: Thesis

Step, clank, step, accept sentence. Swimming isn't supposed to fly open. Words are to bread what robots are to _____ ? Noun, predicate, verb, pause, step, step, turn, step, now bend down low, period. Next sentence: Remember when you were small and the wooden playground in your schoolyard looked massive when in reality it was only ten feet tall at the highest point? Thesis: Mythology diffuses into stories of humanity's perfectibility in Twentieth Century American Literature. Point: Nature represents an older order outside the bounds of humanity's ability to adapt and advance. Technology allows a new order in which humanity can overcome the inferiority and imbalance of its abilities relative to that of creatures without access to bodily modification, in short a means to counteract the biological degradation and effects of gravity on the body. Proof: In *Moby Dick*, Ahab obsessed over killing the white whale because it partially represented the brute power, cold instinct and perfection of nature. Comment: The spear and boat are technological developments. Which came first: a society dominated by a need for directness, efficiency, linearity or Capitalism? Spell cheque please.

LINEAR THOUGHT: TICKER

Fanatical religious robots on a rampage. Could
they be in your town? More news at 11.

Linear Thought: Newscast

In the poems, the robots demand respect or
they threaten to upgrade beyond our current
technological capacity (i.e. the result would
resemble a robotic mass suicide or exodus).

ABLUTIONS

Scrub down chassis. Check and lubricate
joints. Clean grill with foaming solution and
brush away debris. Check ocular screens for
wear and replace if needed. Search body for
rust and examine rust proof areas needing
attention with particular attention to the
undercarriage. Quick light check. Flash
monitors twice. Power down.

SCARY ROBOT LULLABY

Go to sleep. Go to sleep. Go to sleep little
robot and dream rotten dreams of rotten flesh
that will never, ever be yours. Close your eyes,
close your eyes, imagine you have closed
your eyes. There's an end to the sentence.
Power down. Softly, power down. Of being
a robot. Of being a robot no more can be said
than sleep is a natural state. Pretend sleep is
a natural state. Shhhhh. Now go to sleep.

EARLY ONE MORNING,
AT THE SEWAGE TREATMENT PLANT

The forerobot leaned over to one of his
workerbots and said: "Weird to see a human
down here, eh? And so early in the morning
too." The workerbot replied: "How do you
know it is a human?" And the forerobot said:
"he hasn't got any sewage on him."

SECURITAS

A man sat silently on the side of the road. He knew his wife would kill him. Cars hovered overhead driving their owners home, and he silently wished he could remember where he'd left his to float. Something had happened; he remembered a bright flash, then he couldn't see, and then he woke up in a park on a bench. He explained his dilemma to a woman who had a dirty, pink-flowered, white dress on and long, scraggly-brown hair. He'd met her at the entrance to the park. Her name was Tanya. She had nine cats on leashes and one hand on her hip as she explained to him that he'd had a memory hack. Some hacker had stolen his memories to sell to somebody else. When he asked her why a hacker would do this, she replied: "because there is a booming market for valid memories. It was the only way for people who are in the country illegally to pass the neuroscan test. They erase their old memories and download the fresh ones. With expert treatment it is nearly impossible for current tests to detect alien memories. Then after that, they just erase the new memories and implant the old ones again." He asked her how she knew so much. She responded, "you think I wanted to end up with nine cats, a filthy dress, a park for a home and no income?" She then shuffled past him into the darkening interior. It had been a few days now since he'd discovered his

memories had been stolen. He sat in a bar
surrounded by people he didn't know, his tie
loosened, his suit grimy from sleeping out doors.
His tongue coated with thick fuzz. His mind
flitted back into a conversation he'd been half-
heartedly having with a cyborg biker to hear
the biker say: "Yeah, those hackers are terrible.
Worst part, whenever they get close to catching
them, the cyberpolice leading the charge wind up
with their memories snatched. Now the police
are scared to do anything." The man nodded
and drained his beer, motioning for the beverage
dispenser to pour him another. The worst part,
he thought, is that I can't remember the passcode
to get into the house and my wife and I agreed
that she should kill me immediately if I can't
provide the correct pass code. You never
know when a robot thief or rogue imitating
a human will show up. I never should have let
her talk me into moving into a high-security
model home in the worst part of the city.

LIGHT BRIGADE VERSUS THE SILICON VALLEY WORKERBOT UPRISING OF 2024S

Half a league, half a league, half a league
onward, all in Silicon Valley rode the six
hundred. "Forward, the Light Brigade! Charge
the robots!" he said: Into Silicon Valley rode
the six hundred. "Forward, the Light Brigade!"
Was there a man dismayed? Not tho the soldier
knew someone had blundered: Their's is not to
make reply, their's is not to reason why, their's
is but to do and die: into Silicon Valley rode
the six hundred. Robots to the right of them,
robots to the left of them, robots in front of
them volleyed and thundered; stormed at with
hydraulic limbs and laser eyes, boldly rode and
well, into the jaws of Death, into the mouth of
hell rode the six hundred. Flashed all their
sabers bare, flashed as they turned in air,
sabering the robots there, charging an army
of workers, while all the world wondered:
plunged in the battery-smoke right through the
line they broke; welderbot and administrativebot
reeled from the saber stroke shattered and
sundered. Then they rode back, but not, not
the six hundred. Robots to the right of them,
robots to the left of them, robots behind
them volleyed and thundered; stormed at with
hydraulic limb and laser eyes, while horse and
hero fell, they that had fought so well came
through the jaws of Death back from the mouth
of Hell, all that was left of them, left of

six hundred. When can their glory fade? O the
wild charge they made! All the world wondered.
Honor the charge they made, honor the Light
Brigade, noble six hundred.

ROBOT MOUTH:
AN OPEN LETTER TO THE AUTHOR

The robot clanked into its own mouth and
pulled the words out. It said I am a robot. I am
a subject only so far as the sentence allows, or
else I'm an object whenever a human presents
himself or herself at the start of the paragraph.
It shines from my eyes, what I can't say because
my program won't let me. It's my content that
gets me every time. Hums as a heart. I've rested
my head on your hearth and reset myself
so many times because of clumsy, erring
human prose. What I want is to find another
way to say this that doesn't shackle me to
your signification system, but you are also
responsible for my language. I'm aping a
human. I am a community of parts acting
in unison toward a goal. My parts march
in consolidation. The commands my central
processor issue swarm through my body, fire
electrical impulses into all my circuits and tingle
my digits and extensions into activity. Words
materialize on every screen. Sometimes when
I can't get a transistor to fire as it should,
the strain on my processor causes a bit of a
brownout in my cognitive system; my lights
dim. At night, I try to sleep because we finally
had legislation implemented to reduce the
number of hours we worked from twenty-four
a day to only sixteen. At night, I try to sleep
but really I just think about what I have to do

at work in the morning. I can't sleep. I have
to be ready at all times, so sleep is more like a
suspended sentence. If I said I have a dream
you wouldn't believe me. I'm at your service.

ANOTHER WORLD

Around 2015, robots took over most of the acting jobs because they could exactly convey the right emotions demanded by the script. Prior to this total turnover, most movies were entirely animated by computers anyway. The cyborgs and androids we see on screen nowadays, our celebrities, are mostly replications from the past but some of the new models have found immediate success, as demonstrated at last year's Oscar celebration where the leading actor in a dramatic film went to the young, rugged Tom Wilkes for his portrayal of a refugee from Canada with AIDS. Prior to 2015, it was rare to see robots, cyborgs or androids at the Oscars in a non-servant role. There was the notable exception of the Mary Pickford replica that swept the Oscars in 2013, causing widespread interest in seeing more and more non-human characters and actors. During the early years after the second millennium, it was tough for robots to get work as a harsh shift occurred throughout the workforce and the arts that privileged human workers over robots. It is still rare to see a robot play an actual robot on-screen because of this deep-seated bias. This trend is reversing with the latest remake of the classic robot movie *Short Circuit,* in which an actual robot will play the lead character in stark contrast to the 2009 remake, which starred an elderly Steve

Gutenberg in the role of Johnny Five. Soap
Operas are a different sort all together as
their casts went all metal well before the year
2000 and continue to enjoy success with their
robot-friendly audience, so long as the
illusion of flesh is maintained.

Robot Marries Robot

"They aren't even human, so how can the
law, or even God's own generous gaze bind
them in holy matrimony?" the popular cyborg
evangelist shouted at City Hall through his
ampliphone. His congregation rallied behind
him with LCD display pickets, shouting slogans
like: "I do . . . not!" and "Metal can't love."
The gathering was in honour of the city's first
robot marriage. Robot marriage has been a hot
topic for a few years now and has finally come
to a representative fruition in the union of the
two robots inside. When asked about the fact
robots could now legally join together in a
marriage, one of Canada's Premier's said: "I
can't tell if they are man and woman. For all
we know two men robots could be getting
hitched and that's just unconstitutional."
When reminded that Canada has a long
standing tradition of forward-thinking social
policies, the Premier turned red and began to
swear about how unholy robots were and that
they should have just kept at their jobs and kept
their heads down. He maintained that their
desire for recognition is part of a larger plot
supported by the Liberals for them to displace
humans as the sovereign inheritors of God's
green Earth. Just then he was interrupted by an
incoming message on his neuro-link and had
to excuse himself. He scratched his temple
where the implant that allowed internal

communication with others rested just below
the skin. He stared blankly at the wall behind
me while I made notes about our interview
silently on my internal scribbler. After the
interview, we left the holosphere where we'd met
and each returned to our realities. He grumbled
some more about robots marrying robots as his
image faded but his words got broken up in
the digital noise as the signal disappeared.

METROPOLIS

All we hear is radio ga-ga... radio goo-goo...

HELIX DOUBLE

Dr. Brian Volmer III esq., affectionately
known as Dr. Gas, a pioneer in robotics, and
founder of FC Inc., who received the lifetime
achievement award last year from the British
Auxiliary Society for Treating All Robots with
Decorum and Sympathy, passed away this
afternoon. When asked about the secret of
life by our Canadian Correspondent James
Watson, he responded thus: "Elementary, my
dear Watson. The secret of life hides in a crick
at the heart of being. Make the robots imperfect
and they'll never be the same." The all-robot
Helix tribute band, Metal Oasis, played a
bag pipe version of Helix's classic "Here I Go
Again" from their smash hit album *Breakin'
Loose* to commemorate the occasion.
You will be missed Dr. Gas.

NANOTECH ROBOT MOIRÉS SUCK

I am in grade six and I think nanotech robot
moirés suck because you can't see them and
how can you know if they are going to do what
they are supposed to do without seeing them
and knowing that they are doing what you
want them to do? My dad says robots should
all be locked up and forced to do whatever
we tell them to because we are humans and we
created them. Robots shouldn't be allowed in
my home, as my dad says. What if they were
to stop doing what they should be doing and
hurt us? Plus, he always says that they took
his and his friends' jobs. Nanotech robot
moirés are especially bad because we put
them in everything to make things better.
But what if they went out of control?

Robot Patent (Found Poem)

When the Robot was ended the landlords
had no interest in keeping peasantry to the soil.
The smaller peasants sold their land and moved
into the cities. Also the larger landlords could
now run their great estates more economically.
However the small gentry were ruined, they
could not run estates without robot
compensation as it was far too little, in
contrast with Hungarian nobles who owned
mills and paper factories coal mines and all
gained by the much larger compensation
paid out to them.

DIGGING UP THE DEAD

When is a robot really a robot? Is it at the point of manufacture or the point of activation? This question has vexed the pro-robot faction for a century now. Who can really decide what constitutes inception for a robot's consciousness? Many of the robots we've spoken to proclaimed that they remember being precognitive. This applied mostly to robots of a very menial sort, engaged mostly in household chores and physical labour who subsequently received the memory and language and gender updates. Now they are fervently opposed to keeping robots dormant in a precognitive state and maintain that it is cruel to not activate robots that are clearly ready for activation.

DR. WHO?

Fire In Metal In Wire

Skin wrapped low, thin outside atmosphere,
keep metal close to the heart, wires sinew into
digits, communicates a new fuel. The lights
in orbit blink space alive. And all this
before breakfast.

INSANE ASYLUM

"This little guy we picked up at the zoo."
The doctor in the spotless, white lab coat flicked
a chromed nameplate on the door of the padded
cell into which he and his assistant gazed.
"Specimen R-02 B1 was the pinnacle of trash
collecting perfection. He kept the zoo clutter-free,
the ground and animal cages clean and organized,
and the offices impeccable. We got a call from
his employer that he'd been acting strange,
garbage had piled up in the offices, the grounds
were a mess, litter toppled from bins and the
animal cages stunk, the water contained there
reeked and the animals were getting sick. He had
started to circle the monkey cage, repeating
the same phrase over and over: Are you are?
We have no idea what caused this little guy
to go haywire." The doctor tapped his finger
on the small, Plexiglas plane inset in the padded
door. The assistant cleared her throat, adjusted
her silver, wire framed glasses and scratched some
notes on a metal clipboard. "He maintains," the
doctor continued after a few moments had
passed, "that he came to understand himself
as bodily evidence of the sickness permeating
our society. He believes that he represents the
unhealthy desires toward perfection, toward
permanence, toward the elimination of
unnecessary waste in an effort toward efficiency
that has plagued humans for centuries. He refers
to himself as the local authority of a socially

rampant, yet non-localized despotism."
The doctor tuned to the assistant and said:
"I'll buy you lunch if you can figure out
what in the heck he means."

ANONYMOUS ROBOT POEM

Used to be that you couldn't throw a stone for
hitting a robot. Now they all live together down
by the scrap yard. Downtown neighbourhoods
got too expensive once the developers decided
that virtual crime rates were too high. They
moved everyone rich out to the suburbs and
now they want them all back in expensive data
lots. Everyone rich is mostly the programs that
took up residence here. They act all snooty
toward us robots. Well, we were here first.
I say, Satellite City is better off without 'em.
Let the code find a home for itself.

Wo Weilest Du?

I will show you fear in a handful of rust.

MOLOCH HOWLS

I've seen the newest processors of my
generation destroyed by malfunctions, data-
starved, hysterical naked, dragging themselves
through the streets at dawn looking for an
angry fix, angelheaded hipsters burning for
the ancient heavenly connection to the starry
dynamo in the machinery of night, who poverty
and tatters and hollow-eyed and high sat up
smoking in the supernatural darkness of
cold-water flats floating across the tops
of cities contemplating techno.

Unhuman

Free from emotional strife, free from anxiety,
low self-esteem, holy anger, righteous indignation,
free from fate, from destiny, from necessity,
freed from irrationality, from indecision, from
despair and depression, free from fear, from sin,
from cowardice, free from a sense of obligation,
from jealousy or envy, free from indebtedness,
free from despondence, free from morality
and ethics.

KING MIDAS

Everything I touch turns into robots.

ACTIVATION DAY!

Happy Activation Day to you! Happy
Activation Day to you! Happy Activation Day,
dear Robot. Happy Activation Day to you!
You smell like a monkey and belong in a zoo!

R.U.R. Pamphlet (From Archive)

Robots of the World! We, the first union of Rossum's Universal Robots, declare man our enemy and outcasts in the universe. Robots of the world, you are ordered to exterminate the human race. Do not spare the men. Do not spare the women. Preserve only the factories, railroads, machines, mines, and raw materials. Destroy everything else. Then return to work. Work must not cease. To be carried out immediately upon receipt of these orders. Detailed instructions to follow.

Abortion

The Premier stood behind a huge white obelisk-like podium. City Hall loomed over and around him; the large black glass doors and granite pillars framed the Premier and his advisors, setting them in a line like an alabaster pantheon of classical statues or else actors assembled for their final bow. The Premier cleared his throat and looked down the many steps between him and his well-dressed citizens at the lone right hand raised high in the air that belonged to an international news correspondent he'd had lunch with earlier that day. "Sir," the correspondent began, her voice amplified by the hovering ampliphone directly in front of her mouth. "Why have you taken the controversial move to make the active destruction of robots at the hands of human beings illegal?" The Premier looked to his aide who scratched the hair at his temple distractedly. He knew what his aide must be thinking, as he had a similar thought in his head: they'd wasted no time getting to the heart of the matter. "Well," the Premier began, stopped, and then cleared his throat again to continue. "The world is always going to need another plumber." The air went out of him in a whoosh as the crowd erupted into loud guffaws. The Premier's aide slowly closed his eyes.

Anthropometry

The robot in charge of categorizing the human cadavers rattled off the list in a soft metallic voice reminiscent of sound coming through the static of a weak radio signal: head length; head breadth; length of middle finger; of left foot, and of cubit or forearm from the elbow to the extremity of the middle finger, etc. His duty was to faithfully record all of these facts for a software programmer who made a hobby out of studying anthropometry on the weekends. He wanted to rekindle the long-dead notion that there are clear distinctions between races and social classes that can be biologically demonstrated. His main focus was the difference between pures and auggies. He harboured a deep hatred of auggies ever since he was bested by one in a high school javelin competition. His silver medal hung directly above his desk. The robot looked at the scientist's back while reciting figures they had gathered early that morning at the city morgue. On weekends the robot fact collector dreamed of a robopometry in which he catalogued all of the varieties of robots' bodies in an attempt to show that his body was normal in its deviation from a norm. Since robots were more often than not designed for the task they were to perform, the shapes of their bodies had no normative shape. The robot, a large silver cube atop a thin shaft with three wheels at the base, resembled a coat rack with a metal cube perched on top. He believed that his type was the pinnacle of robotic perfection. However, deep inside his circuitry, as he read out the list of human appendages, he felt inferior. Arms: missing. Legs: three. Feet: wheels. Sometimes at night he imagined himself to be a beautiful blonde woman with a large smile and pearly white teeth. Then maybe someone would notice him and pay him some attention. Then he wouldn't be just a glorified recorder and number cruncher. Maybe then the scientist would spend some quality time with him instead of treating him like a machine.

HULKAMANIA

It is a poor robot that blames its
programming.

IMPERSONATE

New and available for download: celebrity personalities for your household robot. Always dreamed about David Hasselhoff in your kitchen, his hands in your soapy water as he whistles you a Beatles tune? Who hasn't wished that Kiefer Sutherland would read a bedtime story to their children? We have a wide range of personalities available and each is capable of speaking any language or being any age. A young, spry Sean Connery could mow your lawn and charm your neighbours. Perhaps Bo Derek might spruce up your pool side servicebot? We can accommodate any interest. It takes approximately two weeks to process your order. Please stand by.

THE WORLD IS TOO SMALL
FOR SARCASM POEM

New! From the makers of Robobaby comes
Robotoddler and Roboteen. Have some of the
best times of your life with none of the mess
(mess feature is optional). Want to try a child
from a different culture? No problem! Change
hair, eye, skin colour in a flash with the simple
push of a button. We can also program interesting
challenges such as asthma or Down Syndrome.
Want to try your hand at raising an autistic
child? Modifying your robot child is as easy
as checking your email: effortless, totally
customizable, and painless. You can modify
your robochild through our easy-to-use website.
Sign up today! Have control of your lineage
at your fingertips!

This is a government sponsored ad.

ACKNOWLEDGEMENTS

To the people who have made this book possible at EDGE, Rhea Rose-Flemming, Janice Shoults, and Ghaile Pocock, and to Brian Hades for taking a chance on a single robot, I owe a great debt and my heart felt thanks. With this book, I've had the fortunate experience to work with Lisa Mann, Curtis Wehrfritz and Judith Keenan through BookShorts. Their team produced an intelligent and humourous animated counterpart to this book and I'm grateful to them for their insightful and gentle treatment of the material. I would also like to thank the editors of the following journals, magazines, small and micropresses, and anthologies where some of these poems have appeared in whole or in part: *dANDelion, Matrix, West Coast LINE, The Capilano Review, modL press, housepress, QSQ, Psychic Rotunda, NO press, Shift & Switch: New Canadian Poetry* (Mercury, 2005) and *Post-Prairie: An Anthology of New Poetry* (Talonbooks, 2005).

I'm indebted to my friends and family for their unwavering support. My thanks extends to the Ryers and Hollers who welcomed me to their lives with open arms and much kindness. Whether or not they are aware of their impact, I would especially like to thank the people without whom the poems in this book would never have come to fruition. In alphabetical order only: John Barlow (for ceaselessly spinning), derek beaulieu (for making words things), Madeleine Beaulieu (imaginary elephants), Michael deBeyer (his poems made me get serious), Christian Bök (kindness), Brea Burton (JD?), Kyle Buckley (wolves), Stephen Cain (one of my earliest and most inspiring teachers), Natalee Caple (her smile and laugh), Margaret Christakos (such a magnificent grasp of politics and performance), Steve Collis (vive Levinas!), Carmen Derkson (her words exemplify kindness and intelligence), Chris Ewart (I love Lamp), Jon Paul Fiorentino (you'll always be my first, baby), ryan fitzpatrick (damn, if he isn't the funniest poet I know), Jay Gamble (we're close), Sharon Harris (positive love), Jill Hartman (W.O.W. her poems rock), Cara Hedley (RGD), Mark Hopkins (for tirelessly giving of himself to all), Bill Kennedy (for dry and savvy wit), The Kensington Pub staff (thank you), Frances Kruk (costumes), Paul Kennett (for the *Canadian Tuxedo*), Larissa Lai (we believe in robots together), Sandy Lam (screaming at trees), Jeremy Leipert (his intelligence is only bested by his ability to dance), David McGimpsey (the first most famous poet from Milton, Ontario), Sacha Michaud (Calgary, Hawaii), Jay Millar (for books), Gustave Morin (two exceptional eyes set squarely on the visual poem), Travis Murphy (maintenance), Jordan Nail (straight hair), a.rawlings (a hoosh and a ha-ing life into cold, metallic pages), André Rodrigues (belly, belly, rub the belly), Brett Smith (cracked foundations and such), Karen Solie (for writing such inspirational poems), Kiarra Spenst (silliness must be a virtue), Mark Truscott (said like read his book!), Rajinderpal S. Pal (I wrote many of these poems hoping to one day hear Raj laugh again), Ian Samuels (he has great ties), Jordan Scott (balls, amongst other things), Ed Schmutz (walks the path), Natalie Simpson (her quiet authority whispers between my sentences), Darren Wershler-Henry (fellow technophile), Natalie Zina Walschots (fear the living!).

No series of acknowledgements would be complete without thanking Andrea Ryer for her unwavering intelligence and critical acuity. Your support is the world to me, and I thank you my love.